W9-CAU-750

AESOP'S FABLES

AESOP'S FABLES

ILLUSTRATED BY
HEIDI HOLDER

Viking Kestrel

To Friends of Animals, Inc.
and to Friends of the Earth

H. H.

The text of this version of *Aesop's Fables* was adapted
by the editors at The Viking Press from several sources,
primarily those of Boris Artzybasheff and Sir Robert L'Estrange.

First Edition

First published in 1981 by The Viking Press
40 West 23rd Street, New York, N.Y. 10010
Published simultaneously in Canada by Penguin Books Canada Limited
Printed in U.S.A.

4 5 6 7 8 91 90 89 88 87
Library of Congress Cataloging in Publication Data
Aesopus. Aesop's fables.
Contents: The cock and the jewel.—The dove and the
snake.—The fox and the grapes.—A laden ass and a horse.—[etc.]
1. Fables. [1. Fables] I. Holder, Heidi. II. Title.
PZ8.2.A254Ho 398.2'452 80-26265 ISBN 0-670-10643-7

CONTENTS

AESOP'S FABLES

THE DOVE AND THE SNAKE

One day a beautiful Dove was preening her feathers beside a pond when she observed her enemy the Snake hiding in the bushes. Keeping her eyes upon the Snake, she failed to notice a Hunter from the nearby town stalking her with a net. Closer and closer he crept, without the Dove's knowing what he was about. Suddenly the Snake slithered into the open, startling the Hunter into dropping his net. The wise Dove, taking advantage of the confusion, quickly flew away to safety.

& *Often good may be drawn out of evil, and even our worst enemies may inadvertently help us.*

THE COUNTRY MOUSE AND THE CITY MOUSE

An honest, plain, sensible Country Mouse invited her city friend for a visit. When the City Mouse arrived, the Country Mouse opened her heart and hearth in honor of her old friend. There was not a morsel that she did not bring forth out of her larder—peas and barley, cheese parings and nuts—hoping by quantity to make up for what she feared was wanting in quality, eating nothing herself, lest her guest should not have enough. The City Mouse, condescending to pick a bit here and a bit there, at length exclaimed, "My dear, please let me speak freely to you. How can you endure the dullness of your life here, with nothing but woods and meadows, mountains and brooks about? You can't really prefer these empty fields to streets teeming with carriages and men! Do you not long for the conversation of the world instead of the chirping of birds? I promise you will find the city a change for the better. Let's away this moment!"

Overpowered with such fine words and so polished a manner, the Country Mouse agreed, and they set out on their journey. About midnight they entered a great house, where the City Mouse lived. Here were couches of crimson velvet, ivory carvings, and on the table were the remains of a splendid banquet. The Country Mouse was placed in the midst of a rich Persian carpet, and it was now the turn of the City Mouse to play hostess. She ran to and fro to supply all her

guest's wants, serving dish upon dish and dainty upon dainty. The Country Mouse sat and enjoyed herself, delighted with this new turn of affairs. Just as she was thinking with contempt of the poor life she had forsaken, the door flew open and a noisy party burst into the room. The frightened friends scurried for the first corner they could find. No sooner did they peek out than the barking of dogs drove them back in greater terror than before. At length, when things seemed quiet, the Country Mouse stole from her hiding place and bade her friend good-bye, whispering, "Oh, my dear, this fine mode of living may do for you, but I prefer my poor barley in peace and quiet to dining at the richest feast where Fear and Danger lie waiting."

& *A simple life in peace and safety is preferable to a life of luxury tortured by fear.*

THE BAT, THE BRAMBLEBUSH, AND THE CORMORANT

A Bat, a Bramblebush, and a Cormorant decided to go into business together. The Bat borrowed money to finance their partnership, the Bramblebush bought cloth, and the Cormorant brought to their venture brass coins. When the three of them sailed abroad to sell their goods, their ship ran into foul weather and capsized. The three merchants escaped with their lives, but all their goods were lost.

Ever since, the Bat never ventures out before night, for fear of meeting his creditors. The Bramblebush catches at the clothes of passersby in the hope of finding its own cloth again. And the Cormorant hovers over the seacoast, searching for brass coins washed ashore by the tide.

& *He who has been struck by great misfortune will remember it forever.*

A LADEN ASS AND A HORSE

A Horse and an Ass were traveling together on a long journey with their master. The Horse's back was bare, while the Ass carried innumerable bundles. Stumbling under his heavy load, the poor Ass cried out to his proud companion, "Please, good Sir, I beg of you to help me carry my burdens, otherwise I fear that I shall die." But the Horse was unmoved by this desperate plea, and refused to share the load.

Soon the little Ass was completely worn out and, stumbling pathetically, finally fell. No matter how valiantly he struggled, he could not get to his feet. Seeing this, their master lifted the many packages from the Ass and flung them across the back of the Horse, who immediately began to groan and wail in self-pity. "Woe is me!" he cried. "What suffering have I brought upon myself! I would not share a lighter load, and look at what has become of me: I must now carry everything alone."

& *The strong should help the weak, so that the lives of both shall be made easier.*

THE FOX AND THE GRAPES

There was a time when a fox would have searched as diligently for a bunch of grapes as for a shoulder of mutton. And so it was that a hungry Fox stole one day into a vineyard where bunches of grapes hung ripe and ready for eating. But as the Fox stood licking his chops under an especially juicy cluster of grapes, he realized that they were all fastened high upon a tall trellis. He jumped, and paused, and jumped again, but the grapes remained out of his reach. At last, weary and still hungry, he turned and trotted away. Looking back at the vineyard, he said to himself: "The grapes are sour!"

& *There are those who pretend to despise what they cannot obtain.*

THE MARRIAGE OF THE SUN

Many years ago, during a very warm summer, it was reported that the Sun was going to be married. All the birds and the beasts were delighted at the prospect of a celestial wedding and quickly set about making preparations for an elaborate celebration.

Above all others, the Frogs were determined to honor the occasion with a festival of singing and dancing. Bedecked in all their finery, they were eagerly awaiting the glorious wedding day when a wise old Toad spoke. "My friends, you might do well to temper your enthusiasm, as this could be an occasion for sorrow rather than joy. For if the Sun alone dries up the marshes so that we can hardly bear it, what will become of us if he should have half a dozen little Suns in addition?"

& *It is possible to have too much of a good thing.*

THE COCK AND THE JEWEL

A brisk young Cock was scratching around on a dunghill for something to eat when he happened upon a glistening jewel. It sparkled with an excellent luster, but not knowing what to do with it, he shrugged his wings and shook his head, saying, "Indeed you are a very fine thing, and if a jeweler had found you, no doubt he would be delighted, but as for me, I would rather have one grain of dear, delicious barley than all the jewels under the sun."

& *What is valuable in the eyes of some may be worthless to others.*

THE HARE AND THE TORTOISE

A Hare taunted a Tortoise because of the slowness of her pace and boasted of his own great speed. "Then let us have a race," said the Tortoise. "I'll run with you five miles, and the Fox yonder shall be the judge." The Hare agreed and away they went. But in his eagerness to win he started off as fast as he could and soon left the Tortoise far behind. The Hare, tired from his exertions, stopped by the way to take a nap, confident that if the Tortoise went by he could easily overtake her. Meanwhile the resolute Tortoise kept up a slow but steady pace and plodded along. The Hare overslept and awakened to find, when he arrived at the goal, that the Tortoise had reached it just before him.

& Perseverance and determination compensate for the absence of natural gifts.

THE STAG AND THE HOUNDS

A Stag one autumn day came to a pond and stood admiring his reflection in the water. "Ah," said he, "what glorious antlers! But my slender legs make me ashamed. How ugly they are! I'd rather have none at all."

The Stag was soon distracted from his vain musings by the noise of huntsmen and their hounds. Away he flew, leaving his pursuers a vast distance behind him. But coming upon a thicket, he became entangled by his antlers. He struggled to free himself as the baying of the hounds sounded nearer and nearer. At last he thought, "If I am meant to die at the fangs of these beasts, let me face them calmly." But when he ceased to tremble, he found his antlers had come free.

Immediately he bounded away, delighting in his legs, which carried him far away from danger. As he ran, he thought to himself, "Happy creature that I am! I now realize that that on which I prided myself was nearly the cause of my undoing, and that which I disliked was what saved me."

& Look for use, before ornament.

ABOUT THE BOOK

The paintings for *Aesop's Fables* were drawn
in pencil on Arches Special watercolor paper.
They were then traced with India ink, using pen
and brush. Watercolors were applied to the
line drawings by brush and sponge.
The art was camera separated and printed
in four colors. The text type is
Monotype Poliphilus.